Murder at Outpost 22

This story is a work of fiction. Names, characters, places and incidents are either the works of the author's imagination or used fictitiously. Any resemblance to actual events, locals or persons, living or dead, is entirely coincidental.

Murder at Outpost 22

The dry soil crumbled through Colton's fingers as he pulled the orange root from the ground. He dusted off the dirt and inspected the vegetable. Satisfied with its size and texture, he placed the food into a basket. The blue sun that heated the planet Grell poured down over the lush, green land that Colton called home. It wasn't much, just a small hut on a few acres of land, but that was all he could afford on an investigator's salary. It didn't matter, his needs were few.

Colton pulled the last root from the ground and briefly inspected it. He stopped when he heard footsteps behind him. He stood and his light-green reptilian body arched around to see who was coming. Colton recognized the visitor's scent. It was Larn. The Grellian bureaucrat walked confidently toward the inspector, flicking his tongue every few seconds. Colton sighed. He hated seeing that primitive trait in his fellow citizens. It reminded him how close they were in their evolutionary development to the critters that still crawled on all-fours.

"Good morning, my friend," said Larn. The administrator wore a dark-blue suit over his scaly body and he carried a satchel over his right shoulder. Colton despised the clothing fashion that was picked up from Earthlings. "They look delicious," said Larn, pointing to the vegetables in Colton's basket. "Though I prefer to eat something with some meat on it." Larn stopped and offered a hand. Another Human custom. Colton shook his hand before he picked up the basket and walked toward his hut.

"I wasn't expecting any visitors today," said Colton. Larn walked beside him as they left the garden behind them. Colton opened the back door of his home and held it as Larn entered first. The host placed the basket on a small tabletop and faced his boss. "What do you need, Larn?" he asked.

Larn laughed. "Always the diplomat, Colton." He opened his satchel and handed his friend an electroreader. Colton reluctantly took the device and turned it on. "We have an assignment for you. It shouldn't take long." Larn's tongue flicked out more often when he spoke. "The Council thinks you are the best investigator for the job."

Colton read the data on the device. He shook his hand and handed it back to Larn. "This is a Human case," he said. "Let the Humans handle it."

"A Human investigator might not be impartial," said Larn.

Colton turned his back on his boss and began washing the orange vegetables in a stone sink. The water flowed over the food and cooled his warm hands. "I'm not ready to come back yet."

"You need to get back to work, Colton," said Larn. He gently placed the electroreader onto a counter near the sink. "You've been away long enough." His voice rose with noticeable agitation. "You can't hide out here forever."

Colton spun and glared at Larn. "It hasn't been that long." He paused and took a deep breath. "It hasn't been long enough." They stared at each other for a moment. Colton took a cautious step forward. "The truth is I don't know if I want to come back. Not after what happened." He shook his head.

Larn spoke in a softer tone. "You did nothing wrong. You weren't even charged with anything. As far as the AIP is concerned, you did your job to the best of your ability." He placed a sympathetic hand on Colton's arm for a moment. "No one blames you for what happened."

"I blame myself!" shouted Colton, as he backed against a near wall. "If I hadn't been so sure I was right, an innocent Grellian wouldn't have died in prison. My pride got in the way. I never really considered other suspects. It took his suicide for me to start looking in the right direction." Colton felt his heart pumping. He closed his eyes for a moment to calm down.

"Anyone could have made the same mistake," said Larn. "There was a strong case against him. His on-going feud with the victim, his DNA at the crime scene, his lack of an alibi. They were compelling facts."

"But he didn't do it," said Colton.

Larn nodded. "And eventually you found the one who did." The administrator rubbed his hands together. "That kind of case is difficult to get over, but you need to move on. You need to take this case and solve it. I know you can. So, does the AIP."

"I can't do it," said Colton. "I don't have it in me anymore. You'll need to get someone else." He walked across the room and opened the back door again. He held it open and stared at Larn. The administrator didn't move. "Please, just leave me alone," said Colton.

Larn sighed. "You have a fine home here, Colton. Don't make me remind you that you are an employee of the Alliance of Independent Planets, and as such, we pay you your salary. It would be a shame to lose such a nice home."

"You're blackmailing me?" asked Colton.

Larn shook his head. "No, I'm just reminding you of your responsibilities." He moved toward the counter and picked up the electroreader. Larn handed it back to Colton. "Your shuttle for Outpost 22 leaves tonight. You will be on it. Study this well and May the Light of Grell guide you during this investigation." Larn exited the hut without looking back. Colton watched him walk away until he was no longer in sight. The investigator turned the device back on and reread the data.

****

Colton carried a backpack over his right shoulder as he hustled through the terminal. He glanced at the scrolling, digital messages that flashed flight information on billboards. He rushed to the military platform where two pilots in dark green uniforms were waiting for him. Colton showed them his credentials and they led him to their spacecraft.

The investigator sat alone in the passenger section of the ship as the pilots entered the cockpit. Though he had read the information several times already, Colton reviewed the facts of the case again. A Human engineer on a space station was found murdered by the station's security chief. The station was Outpost 22, a repair and refueling port for AIP ships. A small crew, led by Captain Julie Raven, operated the facility. Colton had limited information on the crew in his report, and he knew he would have to research them further during the investigation. He strapped himself into his seat and turned off the electroreader.

The cabin shook as the ship took off. Colton held his breath for a moment. Space travel was one of many things the investigator hated, along with sleazy criminals, AIP bureaucracy, and dealing with Humans. Colton despised the way Humans looked at members of other species. Despite being a founding member of the AIP, Earthlings looked down upon their galactic brothers, whom they rarely understood. Arrogance was a common Human trait, one that made working with them nearly unbearable for Colton.

The turbulence subsided. Colton unstrapped himself and leaned back in his seat. The trip would take about 6 hours, so he closed his eyes and slowed his breathing. The pilots were Grellian, so the high temperature in the cabin was perfect for Colton. He thought about his parents and remembered their joy when he earned his investigator title. It took years of field work and study, but he finally got the job he wanted. His closure rate was the best in his unit and he had been very satisfied with his life. Until his last case. Colton guessed that Larn was right. It was time to try to move forward after nearly three months of self-imposed solitude.

Colton felt his stomach grumble, so he visited the kitchen section of the cabin. There he found a refrigerated container with live insects and fresh vegetables. He helped himself to three live winged-creatures and two orange roots. The insects were crunchy but bland, while the root had some spice to it. He finished eating and re-read the case file again. There were crime-scene photos taken by the security chief that showed the prone body on the floor. The victim's face was battered and blood was visible on the console above the body. Colton had investigated plenty of murders during his career, but Human murder cases seemed to have a level of brutality that could make even a seasoned police officer queasy.

Before he left home, Colton downloaded several journals and books onto the electroreader to help pass the time on his voyage. He put aside the report and read the pages of a spy novel written by an Earthling several hundred years before. Human entertainment was the only thing about Earthmen that Colton found intriguing. Despite their many faults, they did possess incredible imaginations. This story was about a secret agent trying to prevent a madman billionaire from attacking a country called Russia with nuclear weapons. Colton had only a vague knowledge of that place from other stories, but he knew that it was a nation of some importance. Colton found the primitive threat of nuclear annihilation comical by current standards, but back then it was a terrifying reality for Humans. Those crude weapons would be no match for the AIP's advanced technology.

Colton got so lost in the story that he didn't realize how close the ship was to its destination. One of the pilots walked into the cabin and sat down beside him. "We're nearly there, Investigator," said the pilot. Colton looked at him and nodded. He began to pack up his things and put them in his bag. "How long will you be on the station?" asked the pilot.

Colton shrugged. "That depends on how my investigation goes. But I hope it's not longer than a few days. A week at most." The pilot nodded and reentered the cockpit. Colton took a deep breath and tried to prepare himself for the task ahead. He knew he had to work again to get past his recent disaster, but he wished it didn't have to be a Human case. He felt enough pressure without having to deal with them.

An alarm blared in the cockpit! Colton rushed forward to find out what was wrong. The two pilots were pressing buttons and speaking quickly. Colton saw two ships on the radar in front of the pilots. The crafts were closing in fast. "They must have been hiding behind that small moon," said one pilot. He turned a knob and spoke into his helmet's microphone. "This is AIP shuttle *Darrow* on official business. Please identify yourselves." He repeated the message twice but the ships did not respond.

The crafts fired laser weapons at the shuttle. The concussions sent Colton tumbling back into the passenger section. He scrambled into a seat and strapped himself in. He was still close enough to the cockpit to see what was happening. The shuttle fired back but missed the targets. The smaller ships looked faster and more maneuverable than the *Darrow*. They continued firing their weapons. Consoles around Colton exploded and steam poured from them. The pilots sent out a distress call as they continued firing at the assailants.

The shuttle continued to be rocked by laser blasts. A small fire started in the cockpit, but one of the pilots quickly put it out. The shuttle rolled from side to side to dodge the laser-fire, and Colton felt his stomach tighten. His head bounced. It took all of his will to not vomit. He could faintly here the conversation between the pilots. They continued to issue their distress call as they recorded their activity into the ship's communication logs.

The *Darrow* finally caught a break as one of the attacking ships flew directly into their gunnery range. The shuttle fired at the craft, and it exploded in a brilliant display of light, leaving just one attacking spaceship. It was now a duel between the damaged shuttle and the untouched warship. The *Darrow's* pilots were shaken, but they remained focused. The Grellian instinct for survival was a strong one and these two young soldiers displayed admirable courage. Colton closed his eyes and prayed to the Grellian god Sarka that the Light of Grell would guide the shuttle to safety.

A direct hit on the *Darrow's* nose caused the main power to fail. Backup lights turned on inside the shuttle, but the craft's propulsion slowed. Black smoke billowed out underneath the ship. The pilots' pleas for help became desperate. Colton also saw that the pilots were having trouble steering the craft. The warship was lining up another shot when the radar suddenly showed another ship approaching. It was an AIP fighter craft and it rushed toward the scuffle.

Before the enemy ship could take another shot, the AIP fighter fired two missiles that destroyed the craft on impact. The *Darrow* pilots sat back in their seats and let out long sighs. Their hands were shaking as they nodded toward each other. Colton heard a voice from the AIP fighter give the *Darrow* landing instructions. The investigator thanked Sarka for his help as the *Darrow* followed the fighter toward Outpost 22.

The shuttle bounced to an uncomfortable landing inside a bay on the station and skidded to a stop. Smoke and steam from damaged consoles and electronic equipment poured out of the craft after the pilots opened the hatch. Colton followed his fellow Grellians to the exit. The heavy stench of Human sweat quickly filled Colton's nose, so he took a bottle out of his bag, poured a few drops of clear liquid onto his fingers and wiped them under his nose. He discreetly put the bottle back into his bag and prepared to meet the Humans.

A Human female in an AIP uniform stepped forward with an extended hand. "Welcome to Outpost 22," she said, smiling. Colton briefly shook her hand. "I am Captain Julie Raven." She pointed toward a Human male who stood behind her. "This is Commander Nathan Ward, my executive officer." The man politely shook Colton's hand. There was moisture to his skin that revolted the investigator. Ward remained quiet. Colton had trouble keeping his eyes off of the man's mustache. It was a thick, black, hairy mass that resembled the caterpillars that used to exist on Earth. Colton kept waiting for it to crawl off of the soldier's face.

Raven turned and nodded toward a second Human male who stood at attention behind her. "This is our security chief, Anton Ladzik." He repeated the friendly gesture but his expression showed that he was not happy to greet this visitor. Ladzik was taller than Ward and looked more intimidating to Colton.

The investigator took his electroreader out of his bag and handed it to Raven. She looked over his credentials as he spoke. "My name is Colton. I am a criminal investigator for the Alliance of Independent Planets." He paused as Raven handed the electronic device back to him. "As you know, I am here to investigate the murder of Chief Engineer Daniel Ross."

Raven started to walk away from the landing deck and everyone followed her. "Yes, we are aware of your assignment. I'm sorry it got off to such a rough start. But rebel activity in this sector has greatly increased lately." She led the group to an elevator platform. They all stood on the lift and it rose slowly to another deck. Colton got a glance of the fighter craft that rescued the *Darrow* as the Human pilots exited the ship.

"Thank you for your assistance, Captain," said Colton. "I wasn't sure our shuttle would make it here in one piece." He stood firmly still next to her as the others on the platform stood behind them.

"I'm glad we could help," said Raven. Her voice was soft but firm, like a mother speaking authoritatively to her children. "We have arranged quarters for you and your pilots. After your long trip, you must want to relax for a while. Commander Ward will show you where they are." Ward nodded in agreement.

The elevator came to a stop and Raven confidently walked forward. Ahead of them were several work stations manned by AIP soldiers. Colton guessed that this was the station's bridge. Raven took a position behind a large computer console. Colton examined the room. It was a state-of-the-art AIP facility, with all the latest gadgets and computer equipment. The investigator only had a cursory knowledge of such things, but he had to admit that the room was an impressive sight.

Ward stepped forward and hit a button on the elevator's console. The lift began moving again and Colton watched the heart of the station disappear. A few seconds later, the platform came to another halt. "Your quarters are this way," said Ward. He and Ladzik led Colton along a gray, metallic passageway lined with several doors that were adorned with three-digit numbers. The group stopped at room number 265. Ward typed a command on the door's electronic lock and the door slid open.

Colton followed his hosts into the room. Though Spartan by AIP standards, the room was far nicer than any in his home. Colton saw brand new furniture, including a reading desk with a chair, and several shelving units decorated with Human paintings and sculptures. The bed in the middle of the room was bigger than any Colton had ever slept in. The door to a small bathroom in one corner was open and he could see the tiny sink and the marble toilet. He was deeply impressed with his quarters but he didn't want the soldiers to know it. The only disturbing aspect of the room was the entrenched smell of Human sweat. Though it was everywhere on the station, it was stronger in this tightly enclosed room.

The investigator put his bag down on the floor beside the bed. Despite his fatigue, he was eager to get this probe started. "I'd like to return to the bridge, if I may," he said to Ward.

The commander looked surprised. "You can, if you like. I thought you would want to unpack and rest first." Ward's voice quivered a bit and Colton wondered how much experience he had with other species. There was a clear apprehension in his tone. Ladzik remained quiet. The security chief's constant scowl was evidence of his dislike for the investigator. Colton wondered how much of a problem that was going to be during this investigation. His job was difficult enough without having to deal with that kind of nonsense.

The investigator removed a scanner from his bag before zipping the bag closed. "I'm well rested and I can unpack later," said Colton. He moved toward the door with the small device in the palm of his hand. "May we get started?" he asked. Ward nodded. "Thank you," said Colton. He followed the men back to the elevator at the end of the hall. They rode the elevator back down to the bridge. Colton stepped off first and marched toward Captain Raven.

The commanding officer seemed surprised. "Are you settled in already?" she asked, as she took a slow step away from her console.

Colton forced a smile. "I'm as settled as I need to be." He glanced around the room for a moment. He noticed the uneasy expressions of the crew members. Having an investigator in their midst must have been aggravating for them. His eyes settled on the captain. "This station resembles the early Mars facilities your people built. Very open and sturdy. Good use of space." He paused, hoping the flattery would ease some of the tension. "Very innovative."

Raven smiled. "I'm glad you like it." She moved closer to her guest and quickly ran the fingers of her right hand through her short, brown hair. "I had the temperature raised a few degrees. I hope you find it comfortable." She was clearly sweating, and Colton noticed that most

of the other Humans were too.

"Thank you, Captain," said Colton. "I appreciate that." They stood in silence for a

moment, both trying to read the other. "I'd like to see the crime scene," said the investigator, as

he turned and broke the stalemate.

Raven circled around him and addressed her executive officer. "Commander Ward, you

have the bridge." Then she addressed her security chief. "Mr. Ladzik, please join us." Ward

followed her orders and Raven and Colton reentered the elevator where Ladzik was standing.

The lift took them down three decks. Raven stepped off first, guiding her guest to the area where

the body was found.

A forcefield surrounded the crime scene. "Security Chief Ladzik put up the forcefield

after securing the scene, per AIP regulations," said Raven. Colton nodded and asked her to

remove it. Raven typed a command on her wrist communicator and the forcefield vanished. "No

one else has touched a thing." She folded her arms in front of her chest. "Everything was done by

the book."

Colton glanced at her. "I'm sure it was, Captain," he said. The investigator turned on his

scanner and waved it over a console. He saw splatters of dried blood on the machine. "What can

you tell me about the victim?" he asked. He kept his eyes on the machine as the scanner

collected data. A reading showed that the dried blood matched the DNA records of the victim.

"Ross was a respected and valued member of my crew," said Raven. Colton thought her

response sounded rehearsed. "His death was a great loss." She paused and took a breath. "To all of us." Colton peeked over at her and saw her eyes moisten. The captain's hands were tightly clenched.

"Did anyone have any disagreements with the engineer?" asked Colton. He bent down and scanned the floor of the crime scene. The device picked up faint footprints in various sizes, which was not surprising in a heavily-travelled area. He rose and faced the captain.

Raven shook her head. "We have a small crew here, Investigator. Tempers flare from time to time, but nothing that would lead to murder." She pressed her lips together. "I can't believe one of my people did this."

Colton turned off the scanner. "If not one of your crew, Captain, then who else would have killed him?" he asked. Raven glanced down at the floor. "It is unpleasant to think about, but the odds are that he knew his killer." He pointed to the blood splatters on the machines. "This was a vicious attack. Someone surely wanted him dead."

"That seems rather obvious, Investigator," said Ladzik, as he walked toward them. "I hope you can shed more light than that on this case." The security chief stopped a few feet away from them. Colton grimaced. Ladzik's stench was stronger than the others and it made Colton's stomach tighten.

"Mr. Ladzik, what position was the body in when you found it?" asked Colton.

"My report included that information, sir," snapped Ladzik. "Along with photos of the body." Colton glared at him. Ladzik stared back at him for a moment. "The body was face down on the floor. The arms were covering the head."

"Who removed the body?" asked Colton.

Raven answered. "Dr. Baldwin did." She uncrossed her arms and pointed in the direction behind Colton. "He took the body to the infirmary, per protocol, and examined it under the supervision of Chief Ladzik."

"That was also in my report," added Ladzik. He took a step toward the investigator. "Did you read our reports, sir?" Colton nodded. "Then you should already be aware of these facts. Is there some confusion somewhere?" asked Ladzik. His face reddened.

"No confusion, Chief Ladzik," replied Colton. He turned to face Raven. "I don't rely heavily on reports. I prefer to come to my own conclusions." He quickly read some data on his scanner. Without looking up he asked: "May I speak to Dr. Baldwin?"

"Of course," said Raven. She looked at Ladzik for a moment. "Please resume your regular duties, Chief," she told him. "I think we can find the Infirmary on our own." Ladzik nodded, saluted his commanding officer and turned back toward the elevator. Colton heard the lift rise as he followed Raven through the station.

The duo walked in silence through several corridors toward the medical facility. They passed the Mess Hall where visiting pilots and crew members sat, eating, drinking and talking. Colton glanced into the room and saw that the two Grellian pilots who flew him here were among those enjoying the station's hospitality. He wanted to thank them for their bravery, but he didn't want to intrude on the Captain's time.

Raven stepped through the open doors of the Infirmary with Colton on her heels. The investigator watched her stop in front of a desk where a middle-aged Human male sat reading data on a computer console. "Investigator Colton, this is Dr. Paul Baldwin, our one and only medical staffer on the station," said Raven. The physician stood and shook Colton's hand. They exchanged cordial greetings. "Dr. Baldwin has one of the best medical minds in the AIP, which often makes us wonder what he did to get stuck with us," she added with a smile.

The doctor smiled at Raven, as if he'd heard that joke many times. He turned back toward the investigator. "Welcome to our humble home," he said. "Anything I can do to help you, please let me know."

Colton held back a sigh at the Human banality. He forced a smile. "Thank you, doctor. If you don't mind, I would like to see the body."

"Of course, of course," said Baldwin. He typed a command on his computer keyboard and the data he was viewing disappeared. He pointed toward another area of the room. "Right this way, Investigator." The doctor shuffled across the metallic floor and guided his visitors to the morgue area. It was in a separate room through two locked doors.

The temperature was considerably lower in the morgue. Colton wrapped his arms around his body as he began to shiver. Dr. Baldwin noticed his discomfort. "I'm sorry about the cold, but we need to keep the room this way to help preserve the bodies," he explained.

"Bodies?" asked Colton. "Are there more than one in here?" he asked.

The doctor laughed. "Oh, thankfully no. Just Engineer Ross's." He pressed a button on a wall and an inclined drawer slid out of an enclosure. Colton observed the frosty corpse of Chief Engineer Daniel Ross for the first time. The rigid body was face-up and the dead man's eyes were closed. The lips were pressed together and the arms lay stiffly at the sides.

Colton reached down and gently touched the lifeless hands. He lifted them one at a time and noticed the wounds on them. "It looks like he fought back," said the lawman. He saw the doctor nod in agreement. There were numerous other cuts on the face and abdomen. "Whoever did this was extremely angry. This man took a real beating." He let go of the hands and faced the doctor. "Any guess yet as to what the murder weapon might be?" he asked.

Dr. Baldwin shrugged. "Something with a blunt edge." He pointed to the wounds on the face. "Notice the indentations? They are all consistent. He was hit more than 40 times. The killer wasn't just angry, sir. He was in a rage," said Baldwin.

"He, doctor?" asked Colton. "Have you established that the attacker was male?"

Baldwin pressed his lips together. "That'd be my guess." He glanced at Raven. "No offense, Captain, but I can't see a woman overpowering him with this much force." Raven nodded. Baldwin looked back at Colton. "I think the killer is a man."

Colton made some notes in his hand-held scanner before looking up at Raven. "Captain, have you interrogated your crew yet?" He turned off the device without looking at it. Colton kept the machine in his right hand as he waited for an answer.

Raven folded her hands as they dangled in front of her waist. "I questioned them," she replied. "Individually, per AIP protocol."

"Did you take notes?" asked Colton. "Per AIP protocol?" He didn't mean to sound arrogant, but the captain's tone was condescending. Despite expecting that type of behavior from Humans, it still stung him. He knew that she was holding something back and that tact would be helpful, but he simply didn't have the patience.

Raven tilted her head to the right and smiled. "Yes, Investigator, I did take notes. You are welcome to them, but I'd appreciate your discretion. Include them in your report, of course, but please don't discuss them with the crew." She glanced at Dr. Baldwin, who nervously cleared his throat. "I'll drop them off at your quarters later, so you can review them."

Colton tried to match her smile. "Yes, I'd appreciate that." He dropped his smile. "I will interview your crew myself. I'll start in the morning." He looked at his device and scanned some of the data.

"I'd like to sit in on those interviews," said Raven. That sounded like a command. Colton locked eyes with her and studied her demeanor. "Perhaps I can clarify anything that might cause confusion," she added.

The investigator shook his head. "That won't be necessary, Captain," he replied. He saw her lips tighten as her eyes narrowed slightly. "I prefer to talk to them alone. Your presence might hinder their honesty." She started to object, but he cut her off. "Besides, I'm sure you have many duties to attend to. I wouldn't want to take you away from them."

The captain turned her head away from the lawman for just a moment, before she faced him again. "Whatever you think is best, Investigator," she said. She nearly spit the last word out between her gritted teeth. Raven put a hand on the doctor's shoulder. "Thank you for your time, Dr. Baldwin. We will let you get back to work." She nodded toward the exit. "This way, Mr. Colton," she said. Colton thanked the doctor and followed Raven to the hallway.

Once outside the infirmary, Raven spoke again. "Perhaps this would be a good time to return to your quarters and unpack," she said. They walked a few steps without speaking. Colton knew better than to start formulating an opinion about a case too soon, but he strongly suspected that the captain was, at least indirectly, involved in Ross's death. He knew that he would have to be careful, since Humans tended to be fiercely loyal to their superior officers.

Colton let Raven lead him to his room. She stopped in the corridor as the door slid open. "Thank you for your assistance, Captain Raven," said Colton. He forced himself to offer his right hand. She shook it briefly before she turned and walked toward the elevator. Colton watched her enter the lift and disappear. He entered his room and sat down on the bed. The investigator closed his tired eyes for a moment and replayed the day's events in his mind. He took a deep breath and picked up his backpack. Colton took out two folded uniforms and hung them in the small closet embedded in one wall. He removed other items and placed them on the reading desk. Colton spent the next hour putting together a preliminary report for his superiors, which he emailed to them when he finished.

The station grew quiet as the day ended. Colton walked along a deserted corridor, bathing in the emptiness of the facility. He winced from time to time, nearly flinching from the stench in the air. It wasn't just the Human scent; there was a mixture of bodily odors left over by various species who visited the outpost. Colton's trained nose picked up the unique stink of six different alien races. He stopped for a moment and covered his mouth until a wave of nausea passed.

Colton forced his legs to carry him forward. He tried to block out the unpleasant scents by focusing on the visual stimuli around him. However, there wasn't much of that in this ascetically-sterile environment. Humans were known for their great works of art, but Colton could see that the outpost was not a replication of anything artful. The floor was a boring metallic surface, the walls were painted a dull tan, and, unlike his room, there were no pictures or decorations of any kind on them. The investigator wondered why the designers thought so little of this part of the station.

The Grellian turned a corner and saw a shadowy figure heading for him. He rubbed his dry eyes and his focus improved. Colton put a smile on his face as he recognized the chief of security. "Good evening, Chief Ladzik," he said, trying to produce a polite voice. They both stopped a few feet away from each other. Ladzik wore his perpetual scowl.

"What are you doing here, Colton?" he asked, with no hint of respect. "Are you lost?"

The investigator shook his head. "Not at all. I am just trying to see the station for myself." He shrugged. "I like the quiet of nighttime and it helps me to get a better feel for a case if I can immerse myself in the environment." He paused and noticed that the chief's expression had not changed. "Are you on patrol?" he asked.

Ladzik was slowly swinging a small, but thick, piece of dull metal in his hands. The oblong object was slightly longer than his right hand. Colton recognized it as a police baton, used by lawmen to subdue suspects. "Yes, I often walk through the station at night to make sure there is no trouble brewing," he said. He tightened his grip on his baton. "Just trying to keep the peace."

"Where you on patrol the night Ross was killed?" asked Colton. He glanced at the baton again and wondered how many skulls were cracked with it. There was no sign of blood or any markings on the baton, which made Colton wonder if it was under used or just well kept. He guessed it was the latter. He found Ladzik's eyes and stayed focused on them.

"Yeah, like I said in my report that you supposedly read," said Ladzik. He started to say something else, but he stopped as he watched Colton pour some fluid from a bottle onto his right hand and wipe the liquid under his nose. "What are you doing?" asked the security chief.

Colton put the bottle away and smiled. "Sorry. Grellians have a strong sense of smell, and Humans, well, are a bit pungent." He laughed softly. "No offense."

Ladzik cracked a smile. "None taken," he said. "You folks kinda stink too." He composed himself. "I guess we all need to get used to each other." He started to walk again, and the Grellian joined him. "How is your investigation going?" asked Ladzik.

"It's been a bit slow so far, but I'm just getting started." He tried to sound confident as he walked stride for stride with the security officer. "So, tell me, what kind of man was Chief Engineer Ross?" he asked.

Ladzik hesitated, and Colton wondered if he were searching for a rehearsed speech. "Ross was a good officer," he finally said. "A fine soldier and a solid leader. But . . ." his voice trailed off.

Colton stopped and looked Ladzik in the eye. "But what, Chief?"

Ladzik sighed. He appeared to be debating what to say. "Ross was no saint," he said, lowering is voice. Colton kept his eyes on the officer, waiting for more. "He liked to drink. A lot." He started walking again and Colton stayed beside him. "Now, I don't care what a guy does in his off-time, but Ross's drinking became a problem," said Ladzik.

"Did his drinking affect his duties?" asked Colton. He shook his head slightly in disgust at the Human weakness for alcohol. Most Grellians had no such vice. They respected their bodies and viewed their health as a top priority. Drunkenness was considered uncouth and could ruin a Grellian's reputation.

The security chief sighed. "I did have to arrest him once for being intoxicated while on duty," said Ladzik. He rubbed the baton against his right leg. "Ross stunk of booze and he nearly passed out on the bridge. The others in the room were clearly embarrassed. Luckily, for us, it was a slow night and the crew picked up the slack. I practically carried him to the brig."

"Why wasn't he court martialed?" asked Colton.

Ladzik paused. He pressed his lips together. "Raven told me to drop the charges," he said, in a near whisper. "So, I let him off with a warning. He slept it off that night and he was fine for a while." The chief switched the baton to his left hand and lightly tapped it against his left leg. "I did find him drunk on duty again a few more times. But I didn't bother to arrest him. There was no point. I knew Raven would tell me let him go again."

The investigator shrugged. "Why would Raven cover for him?" asked Colton.

Ladzik again spoke softly. "There were rumors that they were romantically involved," said the security chief. "But they never showed it." Ladzik chuckled. "It was the station's worst kept secret."

"Thank you, Chief," said Colton, stopping at the intersection of two hallways. "I think I'll head back to my quarters. Have a good night," said the investigator. Ladzik said good night and continued his rounds. Colton slowly walked along the quiet corridor and thought about the chief's words. Colton wondered if the captain's relationship with Ross should make her a suspect. He couldn't quite decide. But he knew that their coupling opened a world of possible motives for Raven.

Despite his long day, Colton was still wide awake. After he returned to his quarters, he turned on a computer terminal that was built into one of the walls. He typed in a security code to gain access to the station's main database. A list of files and programs appeared on the screen. The investigator selected a folder with the station's security footage. He typed in the date of the murder and chose the time a half-hour before the chief discovered the body. Colton rubbed his chin and observed the activities in the Engineering section.

Colton watched the personnel go through their regular duties. The crew came and went, and nothing unusual stood out. Suddenly, the image flickered and Colton saw the chief standing over Ross's body. The investigator ran the footage back a few times, until he did see something odd. The timestamp of the events jumped a full twelve minutes. He ran back the footage a few more times to make sure he wasn't seeing things. Finally, he couldn't deny what he had discovered: Twelve minutes of footage from the night of the murder was missing.

The lawman shifted his focus to the crew's records. He opened and read the file on Captain Raven first. She received high marks on her evaluations from her superiors. There were accommodations for bravery, notations about her leadership skills, and recommendations for promotions. There were no black marks at all on her record.

Colton reviewed the other crew profiles but did not find anything suspicious, until he read the data on crewman Lee Morgan. The junior engineer had high marks like his fellow soldiers, but Colton noticed that there was a break in his time of service with the AIP. The six-month gap was too long to be a vacation and there was no record of a family emergency. In fact, there was no notation of why he was inactive.

On a hunch, Colton switched to the AIP criminal database. He typed in Morgan's name and military ID number. A report popped up. Morgan was convicted of assault on a superior officer and he served a six-month jail sentence. Colton wondered why he wasn't dismissed from the AIP. He dug further and found a letter from a prominent AIP council member that recommended his reinstatement. The council member's last name was also Morgan. After more research, Colton learned that the councilman was Morgan's father.

The investigator made notes in his recorder about what he had learned so far. He returned to the database and brought up the crew's financial records. He quickly discovered that each of them was receiving 5,000 credits each month above their regular pay. The only exception was Dr. Baldwin. His financial report showed nothing suspicious. Colton also noticed that even though Ross was getting the extra 5,000 credits, his overpayments stopped three months before his death.

The night wore on and finally began to take its toll on the investigator. He rubbed his eyes as he began listening to the crew's personal logs. There were the usual entries about the day-to-day challenges they faced. Colton found nothing in Ross or Raven's logs to suggest a romantic relationship between them, but maybe they were just too careful to discuss it. The others' logs were bland and Colton started to wonder if this were a dead end. Then he heard Tran Hun's reports.

Communications Officer Tran Hun had the most personal logs on file. The first few that Colton reviewed were mild, but as he continued, the investigator came across some fiery messages. Most of them were addressed to Hun's family members. He complained to them about his working conditions, his sparse quarters, the quality of the food on the station, and his interactions with his fellow crew members. Hun also shared his political views with his family, including his opinion that the AIP was treating the rebels unfairly. The officer was not shy about his growing discord with the AIP and his desire to quickly finish his commitment and return home.

****

Colton heard a creaking sound above him. He looked up as the room gradually grew dark. He took a step forward and bumped into something. The lawman touched the object and felt the smooth, round surface. It seemed to be metallic and strong. The creaking grew louder. Colton searched with his hands and felt rows of bars in front of him. He grabbed them and shook as hard as he could, but the object didn't budge.

The room was humid and it smelled like urine and sweat. Colton banged against the bars and called out for help. His voice echoed off of nearby walls, but no one responded. The creaking continued to get louder and the sound moved toward him. Light began to return to the room, allowing Colton to finally see the source of the creepy sound. Above him swung the body of a Grellian. It was hanging by its neck with its eyes bulged open. The reptilian tongue dangled from its mouth. The creature wore the tan clothing of a prison inmate. Colton recognized the face: It was the Grellian whom he had wrongly arrested for murder.

Colton snapped his head back. His hands shook and his face was covered with sweat. The investigator was sitting in front of the computer terminal in his quarters. One of Hun's personal logs was still on display. Colton turned off the computer and rose to his feet. He saw the time and realized that he had been sleeping for nearly two hours. He relieved himself in the small bathroom and washed his face and hands.

The Grellian sat on the floor and lightly rested his head in his hands. From this ceremonial position, he began to pray to his god, Sarka. He asked his deity for the strength and wisdom to quickly solve this case, and he prayed for the safety of his people. Colton finished the ritual and rose to his feet. He took several deep breaths and turned toward the bed when he heard someone knock on his door.

"Come in," answered Colton. The door opened and Executive Officer Nathan Ward stepped into the room. The young man smiled and briefly brushed his black mustache with the back of his right hand. "Mr. Ward," said the investigator. "What can I do for you?"

"Good morning, Inspector," replied Ward. The man offered his hand and Colton shook it. "Did you sleep well?" asked Ward. His smile remained and Colton noticed that the officer seemed less nervous than when they first met.

The lawman nodded. "Yes, I did. Thank you for asking."

They stood silently for an awkward moment. Ward looked around the room as if seeing it for the first time. "I am on my way to the Mess Hall for breakfast," he said. "Would you like to join me?"

The Grellian didn't immediately respond. He kept staring at the man's mustache. Despite its grotesqueness, Colton couldn't stop looking at it. "The main crew usually eats breakfast together," said Ward. "It helps maintain morale."

Colton nodded again and forced himself to look at Ward's eyes. "Yes, it would be my pleasure to join you," he said. Ward stepped toward the door and Colton followed him. They walked through the corridor to the elevator and road it to the proper floor. Colton strolled beside Ward as they approached the Mess Hall.

The noisy room was filled with people. Most sat at the rectangular tables in the middle of the room. Ward guided his guest to the table reserved for the station personnel. There sat Raven, Ladzik and Baldwin. Across from them sat Morgan and Hun. Each had a tray of food in front of them. They ate eggs, bacon, toast and coffee. The smell of the food turned Colton's stomach. He quickly longed for a plate of vegetables and live insects.

Raven rose from her seat when she saw the new arrivals. "Good morning, Investigator Colton," she said. "Did you sleep well?" she asked. Colton nearly laughed and wondered if everyone was really concerned about his sleeping experience. He politely nodded at Raven. "Good," she replied. "You know Security Chief Ladzik and Dr. Baldwin," she continued. She gestured toward the others with her right hand. "This is Engineer Lee Morgan and Communications Officer Tran Hun." The men rose and shook Colton's hand.

"How is your investigation going?" asked Raven.

Colton settled into a seat and watched Ward pour a glass of water and place it in front of him. "Thank you, Mr. Ward," he said. He took a sip of the water and looked over at Raven. "I am making good progress but I do not have a suspect yet." He watched her facial muscles relax, but he noticed that the other crew members appeared tense. He decided to fire the first shot. "Anyone here want to confess?" he asked.

They all looked at each other in confusion, before looking back at him. However, none of them appeared guilty. "I didn't think so," said Colton. He drank more of the water. "I need to let you know that none of you are permitted to leave the station until my investigation is complete." No one spoke but they did trade glances with each other. Colton finished his water.

Raven cleared her throat. "Many ships pass through here every day," she said. "They need our supplies and our repair crews. Are we to suspend operations during your investigation?" she asked. The captain held a coffee cup in her hand as she questioned the lawman. Her hands remained steady and her sharp eyes bore into his skull.

Colton shook his head. "That won't be necessary. Your operations may continue as usual, as long as your crew remains on the station." He paused and watched Raven's stern expression soften. He looked around the room for a moment. "Where are the Grellian pilots who brought me here last night?" he asked. "I wanted to thank them again for their bravery."

Ladzik swallowed some food before he spoke. "They were picked up about an hour ago, by another Grellian ship." He smiled slightly. "Looks like you are stuck here with us." Colton looked at the security chief as the others finished their meals. Slowly, the crew members rose and left the mess hall until Colton and Raven were alone at the table.

The investigator leaned toward the captain. "If you have time now, Captain Raven, I'd like to ask you some questions," he said. "It shouldn't take long."

Raven smiled. "I am at your disposal," she replied. "Ask away."

Colton shook his head. "I thought it might be more appropriate to speak in your office." He rose and waited for her to do the same. Raven finished her coffee and left the cup on the table. She turned and exited the mess hall with Colton directly behind her. Neither spoke as they walked through the corridor, rode the elevator and solemnly entered her office.

The investigator sat across from the captain and turned on a recording device that he brought with him to the station. "This is Colton, special investigator for the Alliance of Independent Planets Office of Investigations," he said into the machine. "I am interviewing Captain Julie Raven regarding the death of Outpost 22 Chief Engineer Daniel Ross." He carefully placed the recorder on Raven's desk halfway between them. "How would you describe the nature of your relationship with the victim?" he asked Raven.

"Chief Engineer Daniel Ross was a fine member of my crew," she responded.

Colton gave her a moment to expand on that, but she did not. Instead, she kept her eyes on him, like a poker player trying to hide a hot hand. "How was your working relationship with him?" he asked.

"It was satisfactory," she replied. Again, she added nothing.

Colton decided to go for broke. "Were you in love with him?" he asked. Raven laughed but did not say anything. Colton nodded. "There are rumors that you and Ross were involved in a romantic relationship. Is that true?" Raven leaned back in her chair. "I must remind you that a question from an AIP investigator must be answered truthfully under penalty of law," he added.

She sighed. "Yes, we were lovers," she said, quietly. Her eyes shifted so that she was looking to her right. "But I don't know if I was in love with him." She peered back at Colton. "Human emotions are tricky, Mr. Colton. Are they not?"

Colton folded his hands. "I find many things about Humans tricky, captain," he responded. "Grellians are more straightforward. We say what is on our minds and we are not as talented at subterfuge as Humans are." Raven laughed. "That was not a compliment," he replied. He paused before continuing. "Were you still romantically involved with Ross at the time of his death?" he asked.

Raven shook her head. "Sadly, no," she said. "That was over some time ago."

"Who ended it?" asked Colton.

"It was a mutual decision," said Raven. Colton noticed the bitterness in her voice.

"From what I understand about your race, love affairs rarely end mutually or amicably," said Colton. He stared at her and refused to let the point drop. "Did he severe the relationship?"

Raven pressed her lips together. Her eyes moistened. "Daniel thought it would be better if we did not continue," she answered. "He was concerned about the impact on our careers." She rose and walked around her desk. She softly rubbed her hands together as she leaned against the front of the wooden table. "I must admit, I miss the sound of his voice. And his touch."

"Where were you during the time of the murder?" asked Colton.

"I was playing cards with Ward and Morgan in my quarters," said Raven.

Her answer was quick and precise. A little too much so for the lawman. He leaned toward her. "Did you kill Daniel Ross?" he asked.

Raven shook her head. "No, I didn't kill him." She looked Colton straight in the eyes. "And I don't know who did." She closed her eyes and quietly sobbed. The investigator didn't know if this display was for show, or a real emotional outbreak. He turned the recording machine off and silently left the captain's office.

****

A half-hour later Colton was back in the captain's office. This time he sat across from Executive Officer Nathan Ward. The young man's moustache was no longer a distraction for Colton, who trained himself to see past it. Colton liked the comfort of the captain's chair and he enjoyed the psychological edge it gave him as he asked his questions. Ward kept tapping his thumbs together as his hands lay in his lap, and the lawman made note of it.

"What did you think of Daniel Ross?" asked Colton, after he turned on the recorder. He watched Ward's face, but the young man's expression remained calm.

"He was a good man," said Ward. He sat up a little straighter in his chair. "A disciplined officer who knew how to get the most out of his subordinates. And he wasn't afraid to get his hands dirty when needed." He leaned back in his chair and took a slow, deep breath.

"You say he was disciplined?" asked Colton. Ward nodded. "I understand that he had a drinking problem. One that spilled over into his duties on occasion," said Colton.

Ward shrugged. "He wasn't perfect," he said. "None of us are. But he was a solid soldier when it counted." He looked down at his lap for a moment. "I'm sorry he's gone."

"You played cards together, sometimes?" asked Colton. It sounded like an accusation.

"Yes, we played cards. He was a great poker player. I learned a lot from him."

"Were you playing cards the night he was killed?" asked Colton.

Ward nodded. "Yes. I was in a game with the captain and Mr. Morgan." The lawman noted that the alibi matched Raven's. The officer rubbed his face with his hands. "I asked Danial to join us that night, but he said he had work to do in Engineering. Jeez, that was the last time I saw him alive." He rocked back and forth in the chair and his body shivered.

Colton asked the question anyway. "Did you kill Daniel Ross?"

Ward snapped his head up and glared at Colton. "No. I didn't." He looked down again. "He was my friend." Colton heard the light sobbing and he turned off the recorder. It was getting harder to distinguish between the theatrics and the true sadness.

****

Engineer Lee Morgan was next. He kept tapping his right foot and it began to annoy Colton. They had been talking for five minutes, but Morgan only gave aggravatingly short answers. The investigator was quickly losing patience with the man. "You were in prison for six months," he said, driving to the heart of his questions. "For assault on a superior officer?"

Morgan sneered. "Yes. So what?" he asked. "I did my time." He folded his arms across his chest and his foot-tapping increased.

"And yet you are still in the AIP," replied Colton. "It's good to have friends in high places, as you Humans say. Isn't it?" He watched Morgan's face redden. "Did you have any arguments with Daniel Ross?" asked Colton.

Morgan shook his head. "No." He paused, as if remembering something. "Nothing substantial," he said. Colton glared at him. "He was my boss. We may have had some small arguments, but that happens when you spend every day together in tight quarters."

"Did any of these small arguments ever get physical?" asked Colton.

The engineer clenched his jaw. "No. I never laid a hand on Ross. Or anyone else here at the station," he said. "Ask around for yourself."

Colton didn't hesitate this time. "Did you kill Daniel Ross?" he asked.

Morgan rose and pushed his seat back. He pointed at the lawman. "No. I didn't kill him," he said. "Haven't you been listening? I never touched anyone on this outpost." He turned and stormed out the captain's office. Colton sighed and turned off the recorder.

****

With the recorder on again, Colton tried to size up Communications Officer Tran Hun. The stoic man was the hardest to evaluate. He sat quietly, barely moving a muscle. Colton decided to try a new tactic. Mirroring Raven's earlier actions, he rose from his chair and circled the suspect. "I know you are unhappy here, Mr. Hun," he said, standing directly behind him.

Hun tilted his head toward his right side. "I am fine here," he said. "No complaints."

Colton forced a laugh. "Mr. Hun, all you ever do is complain. To your crew mates, to your family members, to anyone who will listen." The lawman recited a few lines from a message Hun sent to his parents.

"That is a private communication!" he shouted, finally losing his cool. He stood and faced his inquisitor. "You have no right to pry into my person life! No right at all!"

Colton moved back to the captain's chair and sat down. Hun returned to his seat. "You have no privacy when you transport messages through AIP terminals." He paused and glanced at his electroreader for a moment. He looked back up at Hun. "You've told your family that you don't like it here and you can't wait to get home. You've said that you sympathize with the rebels who are fighting our AIP soldiers. Are you a rebel spy, Mr. Hun'?" he asked.

"No, I'm not," he replied. "That's ridiculous."

"But you sympathize with their struggle," said Colton. Hun did not respond. "It's clear from your messages that you think they are being mistreated. Isn't that right?"

"My political beliefs are none of your business," insisted Hun. He clenched his fists and took several deep breaths. "But if you must know, yes, I think the AIP is wrong the way they treat the rebels. They relocate entire settlements without warning. They cut rations to keep the rich well fed. They demand that homesteaders pay higher and higher taxes without providing them with the most basic of services. Yes, the AIP is corrupt and it needs to change."

Colton sat back in his chair and stared at Hun. "Those are not the common opinions of AIP personnel," he said. "Some might even say your words are inflammatory. Did Daniel Ross think your views were too radical?"

"Daniel Ross didn't give a crap about my political views," replied Hun. "He only cared about getting drunk and chasing pretty girls."

"Like Captain Raven?" asked Colton.

Hun laughed. "You know about that?" Colton nodded. "Yeah she was sharing a bed with him for a long time."

"How did that make you feel?" asked Colton. "Were you jealous?"

Hun shook his head. "Not at all. I am not interested in women that way. I prefer men, and no, Daniel Ross was not my type."

"Thank you for your candor," said Colton. "That must have been hard to share. Still, I have to ask you: Did you kill Daniel Ross?"

"No sir, I did not," replied Hun.

"Where were you during the time of the murder?" asked the lawman.

"I was alone in my room, reading a trashy novel," said Hun.

"Can anyone verify that?" asked Colton.

"No," said Hun. "No one visited me that night. I stayed in my room until I heard the ruckus when the body was found." He sank back in his chair, noticeably exhausted. He closed his eyes and rubbed them with his fingers.

Colton turned off the recorder and dismissed the man. He sat alone in Raven's office trying to piece together everything he had learned so far. He still had two more interviews to conduct, but he wasn't sure if they would shed any more light on the case. The investigator looked down at the notes he took in his electroreader. He wondered who had the motive to kill Ross. *Who would gain the most from his death? No one really hated him. One even loved him. Was he killed by a jilted lover? Did he know something dangerous about someone else? Did he owe someone money? Who wanted him dead?*

The lawman rubbed his eyes as he departed Raven's office. He took the elevator to the proper level and walked toward the infirmary. As station visitors passed by him, he wondered if his focus on the crew was too limited. *Could the murderer have been a guest at the station? If that were the case, then the suspect list just grew exponentially.*

Dr. Baldwin was treating a patient when Colton entered the infirmary. The investigator watched the physician apply a salve to a man's arm. The patient winced as the medication touched his burned skin. "Sorry about that," said the doctor. He wrapped gauze around the affected area and helped the patient to his feet. "See your regular doctor in a few days," he said, as the man departed the room. Dr. Baldwin smiled when he noticed his new visitor.

"Excuse me for the intrusion, Dr. Baldwin," said Colton as he approached. "Do you have a moment to talk?" he asked.

"Yes, I do, Inspector," he said in a friendly voice. Baldwin pointed to a set of chairs and they both sat down. "What can I do for you?" He folded his hands and held his smile.

The doctor's calm demeanor put Colton at ease. "I have interviewed most of the crew," he said.

"And now it's my turn?" asked Baldwin.

Colton smiled. "I don't consider you a suspect, doctor," he said. Baldwin nodded. "In fact, I have a favor to ask of you." The lawman paused and looked around for a moment. Though no one else was in the room with them anymore, he felt like they were being watched. "Please help me find this killer," said Colton.

Baldwin raised his eyebrows. "Certainly, sir. I'll do anything you ask." The doctor leaned toward Colton and spoke in a low voice. "But how can I help you?"

"Just be vigilant," explained Colton. "Keep your eyes open, as you Humans say. If you see or hear anything that might be helpful, please let me know." Colton rose and offered a hand to the doctor. They shook hands quietly like two schoolboys sharing a secret. The investigator departed the infirmary and traveled back to Engineering for another look at the crime scene.

Colton wasn't sure what he was looking for, but he knew that another examination couldn't hurt. He contacted Raven through an intercom in Engineering and asked her to turn off the forcefield around the crime scene. After the field dropped, he used his scanner again as he studied the bloody console. Colton closed his eyes for a moment and tried to imagine the attack. He pictured the violent encounter, heard the crack of the weapon against Ross's head, watched the blood splatter as the victim fell to the floor.

The lawman snapped his eyes open. He shuddered as he looked around. Colton had investigated countless violent crimes during his career, but it never got easier. He tried to distance himself from his victims after he finished his cases, but during them, he had to embrace their experiences to do his job. It always took an emotional toll on him, but this case was even more stressful because he was dealing with Humans.

Colton took a few steps away from the console and paced back and forth in front of it. He pressed his fingertips together and allowed his tongue to flicker. Out of the corner of his eyes, he watched a single crewman in an AIP uniform type on a keyboard at another station. This replacement solider was not on the station at the time of the murder, so Colton did not need to consider him a suspect. The investigator quickened his pace and shook his head. He hadn't found anything new and that frustrated him.

He turned in the direction of the bloody console when he saw something falling toward him. The lawman dove toward the machinery as a barrel of fuel slammed the ground and exploded on impact. His head bounced off his arms as his body crashed against the floor. He blinked his eyes a few times before the darkness overtook him.

****

Colton felt unbearable pain in his head as he opened his eyes. He didn't know how long he had been unconscious, but he found himself looking at the concerned face of Dr. Baldwin. He opened his mouth but only heard air escape his lungs. "Don't try to talk, Inspector," said Baldwin. "You've been in a nasty accident." Colton turned his head slightly and saw Raven and Ladzik standing over him.

The doctor shined a light in Colton's eyes. "You have a concussion," said the physician, as he turned off the small flashlight in his hands. "But you don't have any broken bones." The doctor made a notation in a small, hand-held computer. "You are lucky to be alive. If the fuel had ignited, you and half of Engineering would have burned to cinders."

Colton forced himself to speak. "How did it happen?" he asked. He noticed the tension in the faces of Raven and Ladzik. They knew who did this, or they at least had their suspicions. Ross's killer had tried to murder him, and now he was getting angry. "Tell me!" he demanded.

Baldwin placed a hand on the victim's chest. "Take it easy, sir," he said. He lifted his hand. "You need to rest now. Doctor's orders." Baldwin motioned with his head and Raven and Ladzik followed him to the other side of the room. They spoke too quietly for Colton to hear them. The captain and the security chief then left the infirmary. Baldwin came back over to his patient. "The captain assures me that the incident is being fully investigated," he said.

That did not give Colton any comfort. For all he knew, she may have been in on it. The investigator closed his eyes and replayed that moment in his mind. He didn't remember seeing anyone on the walkway above him, but he wasn't looking up there at the time. He knew that the barrel was quite heavy, so whoever tossed it at him must have considerable strength. Colton wondered if that ruled out Captain Raven.

He slowly sat up. Baldwin tried to object, but he cut the doctor off. "I need to return to my quarters," he said. He rose to his feet and Baldwin helped him steady himself. "I am going to catch whoever is responsible for Ross's murder and this attempt on my life," he asserted. "How do I treat this concussion?" he asked.

"The only thing you can do is rest, but stay awake," replied Baldwin. "I will walk you to your room but you must promise me that you will slow down." Colton nodded. He rested an arm around the physician's shoulder and they gently walked out of the infirmary. Baldwin rode the elevator with Colton and escorted him to his quarters. After the doctor left, Colton eased toward a desk and sat down. He wrote a report and emailed it to his superiors, noting his interviews and his suspicions, but still no firm suspect.

Colton spent two hours rereading the crews' records and listening to their personal logs. His thoroughness did not pay off. He didn't find anything new, so he turned off the computer in his quarters and slowly rose to his feet. His head hurt and there was a ringing in his ears. He was surprisingly tired and he wanted to sleep, but he followed Baldwin's orders to stay awake. The lawman left his room and walked back toward the infirmary.

Baldwin was sitting at his desk and typing data into his computer when the investigator entered. The doctor rose and met Colton halfway through the room. "How are you feeling, Inspector?" he asked. He didn't wait for an answer. Instead he during a cursory examination of Colton's eyes and ears. "Everything looks alright," he concluded.

"Yes, I'm fine now," said Colton. He was still in pain but the ringing subsided. "Do you have a moment to walk with me, Dr. Baldwin?" asked Colton. The doctor nodded and followed his patient into the hallway. Two pilots walked past them and Colton waited until they were out of earshot. "You are the only one on this station that I trust," he said.

Baldwin smiled. "Thank you, Inspector," he said.

Colton quietly shared his findings with the doctor, who nodded from time to time as the inspector spoke. They stopped in front of a supply closet when he finished. "Is there anything that you can tell me, doctor?" asked Colton.

Baldwin shrugged. "Only that the killer didn't leave any physical evidence at the scene, which is quite remarkable when you consider how vicious the attack was." He paused and looked past Colton, as if trying to remember something. "I don't think this was a spontaneous attack," he added. "I think the killer planned to eliminate Ross."

"I agree," said Colton. "Raven, Ward and Morgan all have alibis. That leaves Ladzik and Hun as my only real suspects."

"And me," said Baldwin. "But for the record, I was in the infirmary filling out paperwork at the time of the murder. The logs will show that." He nodded to emphasize his point.

"I have no doubt, Doctor," replied Colton. "As I've said before, I don't consider you a suspect in the murder of Daniel Ross." He let a smile slip across his face. "If I did, we wouldn't be having this conversation." He reassuringly patted the doctor on the shoulder. They turned and walked back to the infirmary. "I think it's time to talk to Ladzik again," said Colton. "Thank you for your help. Have a good evening."

The lawman strolled through the station until he came across Ladzik outside of the Mess Hall. The security chief stopped and smiled when he saw the inspector. "I was wondering when you were going to get to me," said Ladzik. He had his nightstick in his left hand and he tightened his grip on it. For a moment, Colton wondered if he were going to strike him with it.

Colton forced a smile. "You were the one who found the body," he said, stopping a few feet away from Ladzik. "That makes you an unlikely suspect," said Colton. "But still, it couldn't hurt to chat. Right?" he asked.

Ladzik matched his artificial smile. "No harm in that," he answered.

"What were you doing just before you found the body?" asked Colton. "I'm sure you put that into your report, but I would just like to go over that again." He stared into the man's eyes to see if he could detect any deception. He did not.

Ladzik rubbed his chin. "I was on patrol. Everything seemed normal," he said. "I had a brief conversation with a ship's captain who was concerned about some thefts aboard his ship. He asked me for advice." Ladzik shrugged. "I gave him some basic information on how to increase the security on his ship."

"Did this captain know Daniel Ross?" asked Colton.

"I don't think so," replied Ladzik. "Anyway, our talk ended just minutes before I found the body. He wouldn't have had time to commit the crime. And his clothing wasn't ripped or blood stained." Ladzik shook his head. "No, he had nothing to do with it."

"Did you see or hear anything unusual before discovering the body?" asked Colton. "Any yelling or screaming, anything like that?" he asked.

Ladzik shook his head again. "No. And that's why it was so surprising to find him that way," he said. "I didn't hear any disturbance at all." He shifted the nightstick to his other hand. "I immediately secured the scene and called Captain Raven," he said.

"Did anyone act suspicious right before or after the murder?" asked Colton. The security officer said no. "Was there any bad blood between Ross and any crew member?" asked Colton.

"No," said Ladzik. "The crew generally got along, as well as any can, working day and night together in such a small station." He stopped and looked down as if remembering something. The lawman asked him what was wrong. Ladzik scratched his head. "Ross did argue politics with Hun sometimes," he said. "It never got violent. But, I remember now, that they had a big argument the day before the killing."

"Thank you, Mr. Ladzik," said Colton. He shook the man's hand. "You have been very helpful." The inspector turned and walked toward the nearest elevator. The next step in his investigation was clear to him. He rode the elevator to the bridge and was happy to find Captain Raven on duty. She was standing at a console and speaking to Ward.

Colton's heart raced as he approached her. She smiled and asked him what he needed. "I would like to begin a search of the crew's quarters," he said. Her expression soured, as Colton expected. "I am sure it will be beneficial," he added.

"That won't be necessary," said Raven. She nodded at Ward and he walked away from them. "You see, Inspector, we already did that and nothing substantial turned up." She took a few steps away from the console and Colton followed her. "It would be a waste of your time."

"With all due respect, Captain, I did not participate in that search and I would be remiss in my duties if I didn't look for myself," replied Colton. He knew he sounded like a pretentious Human bureaucrat and he hated it, but he didn't trust their efforts.

Raven stopped and glared at him. "I already subjected my crew to an invasion of their privacy. I won't do it again." She pressed her lips together. "Your request is denied. Now, if you will excuse me, I have a busy station to run."

She tried to walk past him but he stepped in front of her. "I was asking as a professional courtesy, Captain," he said. "I don't need your permission to do a search. I have AIP authority to conduct my investigation as I see fit. Now, I don't want to be antagonistic, but if you and your crew will not cooperate, I will call for an AIP security force to board the station and enforce my authority." He paused and let that sink in. He softened his tone. "You and Ladzik can join me in my task to see that I do not disrupt the crew more than necessary."

Raven sighed. "Fine," she said. "Just give me an hour first before you begin."

Colton shook his head. "No, I don't want the killer to have time to destroy any evidence," he said. "I will begin in five minutes. We will start with your quarters." He turned on his heels and marched away before she could object.

****

Raven and Ladzik stood by as Colton dug through the captain's personal items in her quarters. Out of respect for the commanding officer, the inspector carefully moved items aside and put them back as he found them. When he finished, there was no evidence of his search, nor was there any evidence of her involvement in Ross's murder. Colton thanked her and proceeded with his investigation.

Ward's quarters were next. Again, nothing suspicious was found. Colton moved on to Ladzik's room, where he found an odd collection of ancient Earth weapons in a locked display box, but nothing connected to the killing. He also came up empty after searching the rooms of Lee Morgan and Dr. Baldwin. Colton was beginning to wonder if Raven were right. It was looking like an exercise in futility.

The last quarters to inspect belonged to Communications Officer Tran Hun. The young man stood by stone-faced as Colton poked through his belongings. Everything was in order in his room and the inspector was just about to conclude his search when he noticed a loose panel along the wall by Hun's bed. Colton popped open the panel and felt around inside. His right hand encountered a long, metallic object that was curved at one end. He pulled it out and looked at it under the light. The bar was blood-stained and strands of hair were stuck to it.

"How do you explain this?" asked Colton, as he shoved the bar into Hun's face.

Hun turned pale. "I've never seen that before," he said. "I don't know what that's doing here." There was panic in his voice. Colton nodded toward Ladzik, who immediately arrested the young man. "That's not mine!" screamed Hun, as Ladzik dragged him out of the room. "That's not mine!"

Raven shook her head and seemed to be at a loss for words. "I don't know how we missed that, Inspector," she finally said. "Why?" she asked. "Why would Hun do this?"

Colton carefully wrapped a large, plastic evidence bag around the bar. "I don't have an answer for that, Captain." He looked into her wet eyes. "But I will certainly try to find out. First, I need Dr. Baldwin to test the blood on this," he said.

****

The inspector sat across from Hun inside one of the station's holding cells. Hun's hands and feet were shackled and his body shook. "The lab results show that the blood on the weapon we found in your room match the blood of Daniel Ross," said Colton. "The hairs on it are also a match. That is, without a doubt, the murder weapon." He paused before looking straight into the suspect's eyes. "Why did you kill him?" asked Colton.

"I didn't kill anyone!" insisted Hun. He sat back in his seat and closed his eyes for a moment. "Why would I?" he asked, opening his eyes. Beads of sweat slid down his cheeks and his breathing was labored. "I had no reason to kill him."

Colton nodded. "Ladzik told me that you argued with Ross the day before the murder," he said. "And that you two had argued before."

Hun nodded. "Sure, we argued," he said. "Hang around someone long enough and you're bound to get into a fight. But that doesn't mean I killed him." He took a deep breath. "Did you find my fingerprints on the murder weapon?" he asked.

Colton shook his head. "No, we didn't," he said. "But you could have worn gloves."

"So, I was careful enough to wear gloves, but stupid enough to leave the bloody evidence on the bar?" asked Hun. "And why would I hide the bar in my quarters? Wouldn't I have thrown it out an airlock or something?" he asked.

"Maybe you panicked," said Colton. "Or maybe something inside of you wanted to get caught." Hun turned his head and sighed. "It's happened before," said Colton. "That doesn't really matter. We found the weapon in your room. You are guilty."

Hun kicked the table leg, startling the inspector. "That's the way it is with you aliens, isn't it?" he asked. "You hate Humans and you can't wait to see one of us hang." Colton sat back and tried to remain calm. "I know about you, Inspector," said Hun. "We all do. We know about your last case. You were wrong then and you are wrong now. Does that matter?"

Colton stared at the suspect and tried to hide the fact that he was now doubting himself. He folded his hands together. "Tell me, then, Mr. Hun," he said. "If you didn't kill Ross, who did? And why was the murder weapon found in your quarters?"

Hun laughed, which again startled Colton. "Inspector, you have no idea what's going on in this station," he said. "And I'm not going to die for a crime I didn't commit. Not knowing what I know."

The lawman folded his arms. "What do you know, sir?" he asked. "What is going on at this station?"

Hun shook his head. "You wouldn't believe me, even if I did tell you."

"I keep an open mind," said Colton. "Try me."

"We're not just a repair and refueling station," said Hun. He spoke softly and slowly, as if he were afraid of who else might be listening. "We sell weapons and military information to the rebels. Captain Raven runs the operation and we are all a part of it."

The inspector lowered his eyebrows. "So why kill Ross?" he asked.

"He wanted out," said Hun "His patriotism and his conscience got the best of him. But there is no getting out. So, they had him killed."

"Who killed him?" asked Colton.

Hun shrugged. "It could have been any one of them. We were all in on it." He looked down at his hands. "Except, Dr. Baldwin. He knew about it but he didn't help or get paid for it. He isn't that kind of man."

Colton nodded and rose from the table. "That's an incredible story, Hun," he said. The lawman picked up his recorder and turned it off. "Can you prove any of it?" he asked. He locked eyes with Hun and waited for the suspect's reply.

"You are a smart person," said Hun. "I'm sure you've checked our financial records as part of your investigation. Find anything strange?" Hun didn't blink as he looked back at the inspector. "You know I'm telling you the truth. I may be guilty of treason, but I didn't kill anyone." Hun dropped his head. "I'm no murderer."

The investigator left the cell and heard the force field close behind him. He saw Raven and Ladzik enter from the observation room. They both looked worried. "You don't believe that ridiculous story, do you?" asked Raven. Her voice had a slight quiver.

Colton shook his head. "Not at all," he replied. "Hun is just building his defense. Maybe trying to portray himself as unstable in hopes of a lighter sentence. He is the killer. I'm sure of it." He shook hands with Raven and Ladzik. "Thank you for your cooperation during my investigation. I'm going to send my final report now and arrange for my passage home."

****

Colton slept for nearly five hours that night, but he still managed to awaken and appear on the bridge just as the morning shift took over. He was standing next to Ward when the wave of AIP ships arrived and docked at the station. The troops rushed onto the bridge with their weapons drawn as Raven and her crew stood in stunned silence.

"What is the meaning of this?" asked Raven.

Major Jarvis, the senior AIP officer of the arresting soldiers, read Captain Raven her rights. As he did so, Colton approached her with a stern expression. "Hun's story is true, Captain," he said. "AIP officials have long suspected rebel collusion on Outpost 22, but they didn't have the evidence they needed. Not until Daniel Ross was murdered."

Raven took a step toward him, but Jarvis held her back. Colton continued. "You see, I wasn't just sent here to investigate a murder, I was also tasked with proving your crew's treason. I believe I have done both." He nodded at Jarvis and Raven was removed from the bridge, along with the rest of her crew. Colton had just one last thing to do.

The lawman entered the infirmary and found Dr. Baldwin sitting at this desk with an AIP soldier pointing a weapon at him. Colton shook his head at the soldier, who lowered his rifle. Baldwin took a deep breath and let it out slowly.

"You weren't in the infirmary at the time of the murder," said Colton. "There are no logs for that time. But you know that. You knew I'd check up on that, so you lied to me to send me in the right direction. You also know who the killer is, don't you?" he asked.

Baldwin bent his head down so he could rub his eyes against his cuffed hands. "Yes, I know who killed Ross," he said. "You have to understand. It was one thing to turn a blind eye to the seditious activities aboard the station, but I couldn't let a killer go free. That goes against everything I believe in," he said.

"So, what happened that night?" asked Colton.

Baldwin spoke slowly, and Colton could hear the defeat in his voice. "I couldn't sleep that night, so I walked through the station in hopes of tiring myself. I was near Engineering when I heard a loud argument. I couldn't make out what was said, but I could tell that it was serious. I slipped in quietly to see if I could help when I saw Captain Raven attack Ross with the murder weapon."

"Why did you lie about it?" asked Colton.

"I never took any credits from the rebels, but I knew what was happening," said Baldwin. "Raven and Ladzik both reminded me of that fact and that I would go to jail along with the others if I didn't keep my mouth shut. So, I planted the weapon in Hun's room."

"But you had a change of heart?" asked Colton.

"You could say that," replied Baldwin. "After I met you and saw how your investigation was progressing, I knew it was only a matter of time before everything unraveled. I decided not to prolong my agony."

Colton nodded toward the armed solider as Doctor Baldwin rose. The investigator watched them disappear from the infirmary and he wondered if every Human had a price. Grellians were far from perfect, but Colton knew they treasured their honor as much as their lives. Baldwin seemed to be a man of integrity, but even he could not measure up to Grellian standards. *Could any human?* Colton wondered.

****

The blue Grellian sun warmed Colton's face as he dug through the dirt in his garden. He turned as he heard the familiar footsteps behind him. Larn was again adorned in a dark suit and Colton wondered why his boss never varied his outfits. "I was wondering when you would stop by," said Colton. He rubbed his nose and allowed his tongue to flicker.

"I would have been here sooner, but you know how busy the AIP keeps me," said Larn. He stopped in front of Colton and they shook hands. "Wonderful job on the Ross case," he said. "I knew you would solve it. You are the best."

Colton chucked. He reached inside his shirt pocket and handed his boss an electroreader.

"What is this?" asked Larn, as he turned on the device.

"It's my resignation," said Colton. "I'm done investigating crimes."

Larn read the data and turned off the small machine. He stuck it inside his shirt pocket. "What will you do instead?" he asked.

"I've been asked to teach at a law enforcement school," replied Colton. "I can do some good there. Make sure future investigators don't make the same mistakes I've made." He smiled and thought about his transition into the academic world.

Larn nodded. "I'm sorry to see you go," he said. "But I think I understand. Good luck, my friend." They shook hands again before Larn turned and quietly walked away.

Colton watched his former boss depart. He started to whistle as he looked at the orange foods growing in his garden. He knew with hard work and the proper care, he could grow something worthwhile and be proud of it. All he needed was time.

(End)